MY LIFE OFF-KEY

MY LIFE OFF-KEY

Gail Anderson-Dargatz

ORCA ANCHOR

ORCA BOOK PUBLISHERS

Published in Canada and the United States in 2024 by Orca Book Publishers.
orcabook.com

Library and Archives Canada Cataloguing in Publication
Title: My life off-key / Gail Anderson-Dargatz.
Names: Anderson-Dargatz, Gail, 1963- author.
Series: Orca anchor.
Description: Series statement: Orca anchor
Identifiers: Canadiana (print) 2023018491X | Canadiana (ebook) 20230184952 |
ISBN 9781459834798 (softcover) | ISBN 9781459834804 (PDF) |
ISBN 9781459834811 (EPUB)
Classification: LCC PS8551.N3574 M9 2024 | DDC jC813/.54—dc23

Library of Congress Control Number: 2023933534

Summary: In this high-interest accessible novel for teen readers, Jen learns that her mom has been keeping a secret: Jen has a biological father who isn't the dad she grew up with. Now this secret threatens to tear their family apart.

Orca Book Publishers is committed to reducing the consumption of nonrenewable resources in the production of our books. We make every effort to use materials that support a sustainable future.

Orca Book Publishers gratefully acknowledges the support for its publishing programs provided by the following agencies: the Government of Canada, the Canada Council for the Arts and the Province of British Columbia through the BC Arts Council and the Book Publishing Tax Credit.

Design by Ella Collier
Edited by Doeun Rivendell
Cover photography byShutterstock.com/LightField Studios
and Shutterstock.com/Tartila
Author photo by Mitch Krupp

Printed and bound in Canada.

27 26 25 24 • 1 2 3 4

For my two dads.

I miss you both.

Chapter One

The stage lights are in my eyes. I'm so nervous my knees are shaking. But when I clutch the mic in both hands, my voice soars.

I *love* to sing. I've been performing onstage since I was ten. Now, at seventeen, I'm thinking of making it a career.

The high school theater is full of people watching me at this talent show. Mom and my little sister, Ella, are in the first row, smiling up at me. While I'm dressed in black, my favorite color, they both wear bright summer dresses and sandals.

The seat beside Mom is empty. Dad said he would be here. But he isn't, as usual.

I finish my song, and everyone claps. A man in the second row steps into the aisle and tosses roses onto the stage at my feet. Weird. I don't know the guy. He's about Dad's age, balding, wearing all black.

I pick up the flowers and take a bow. Everyone stands as they clap. Mom looks so proud of me, her eyes shining.

I grin as I climb down the stairs to take my seat next to Mom. Before I get there, Ella runs up and hugs my waist. "Jen, you were so good!" she says. Then she looks over her shoulder. "But who is that man?" she asks. "The one who threw the flowers?"

"I have no idea," I say. But I hold up the roses to him, saying thanks.

At that, my mom turns and finally sees the guy. For a moment her smile fades. But then she grins again as I sit beside her. "Jen, that was wonderful," she says. "You sang so beautifully."

I nod at the man in the second row. "Do you know who that guy is?" I sniff the flowers. "Why would he give me these roses?"

"No," she says. "I don't know him." But I can tell she's lying. She looks worried.

"Are you sure?" I ask.

She shushes me as an all-girl hip-hop act starts dancing on stage.

I glance over my shoulder at the man. He's not watching the dancers. He's watching *me*.

I lean into Mom. "Seriously, who is that guy?" I ask her.

"Yeah, who is he?" Ella says too loudly.

Mom puts a finger to her lips to get us to be quiet.

I turn back to the stage, to the girls dancing. But I can feel the stranger watching.

Finally the dancers take a bow, and I clap along with everyone else. Then it's time for the judges to select the winners of the talent show. I sit forward, barely able to breathe. I know I did well. People stood up to clap. But there were so many other great acts.

And then my music teacher says my name, Jen Baker. I've taken third place! Mom hugs me, and so does my sister. I race up to the stage. My music teacher hands me a trophy and an envelope containing a cash prize. "Congratulations!" she says. I would have liked first place, but taking third is great. I placed! I just wish Dad was here to see it.

As everyone claps, I look down at Mom, then at the man who gave me the roses. He's the only one standing as he claps. Even though he's smiling, he looks sort of sad.

Then he turns and heads up the aisle. He's leaving!

I trot down the stairs and run after him. "Excuse me," I call out. But he doesn't turn around. He only walks faster.

I finally catch up to him as he reaches the doors. "Hey, who are you?" I ask. "Why did you give me these roses?"

The man looks past me, at my mother in the front row. She's standing now, facing us. Everyone else is watching the stage as the second-place winner is announced.

"Is that your sister?" the man asks. "Ella, right? How old is she now? Eight?"

Nine, but I don't bother to tell him that. "You know my mom," I say to the man. It's clear she knows *him*.

He nods, still looking toward the front row. "I used to know Sara," he says. Then he turns his gaze to me. "I'm Mike. I—" He stops, like he's not sure he should continue. But then he does. "Jen, I'm your dad."

Chapter Two

I step back and shake my head at Mike. "What are you talking about?" I say. "You're not my dad."

"I'm sorry your mother didn't tell you about me," he says. "But I *am* your father."

I peer at him. He's wearing black jeans and a leather jacket like mine. There *is* something strangely familiar about him. But I know I haven't seen him before.

Onstage, my music teacher announces the first-place winner. As the crowd applauds, Mom rushes up the aisle. She must have told Ella to stay put, because my sister is still in her seat. And I know that look on Mom's face. She's mad.

As Mom arrives, Mike hangs his head, like he knows she's going to yell at him. "Hello, Sara," he says.

"What are *you* doing here?" she asks him.

She *does* know the guy.

Mike waves a hand at the stage. "I saw on social media that Jen was performing tonight. I wanted to see her."

"You follow me online?" I ask.

"Only so I know how you're doing," Mike says.

Mom points a finger at Mike. "You promised you would stay away," she says.

"I did stay away, while Jen was small," Mike says. "But she just turned seventeen. It's time we told her the truth."

"You know when my *birthday* is?" I ask.

"I celebrate every one of your birthdays." He glances at my mom before adding, "I just wish I could have spent some of them with you, Jen."

"We had an agreement," Mom says to Mike.

"You can't expect me to stay away forever," Mike says. "Jen is my daughter."

Mom crosses her arms and looks away. But she doesn't deny it.

My head is spinning. This is crazy. "He really is my dad?" I ask Mom, waving a hand at Mike.

"*Steve* is your dad," Mom says. "He raised you."

"Jen is my daughter too," Mike says.

"*Is* he?" I ask Mom. "Is Mike my father?"

Mom presses her lips together. Finally she nods, like she doesn't want to admit it. "Mike is your biological dad, your natural father."

"When did you and he—?" I do the math. I just turned seventeen, but Mom and Dad were married twenty years ago. So that means— "You had an *affair* with Mike?"

Mom looks back at Ella in the front row and doesn't reply.

"Does Dad know?" I ask Mom.

She chews her lip. "No."

"We should talk," Mike says to me. "If you'd like my number—"

But Mom cuts him off. "She doesn't."

"Maybe I do," I say. "I have some questions to ask." A *lot* of questions.

"You need to stay away from my family!" Mom yells at him. A few people in nearby seats look her way. "Just stay away from my daughter."

Then she waves for Ella to join us. My sister runs up the aisle. When Ella reaches us, Mom pushes her ahead and out the door. "Let's go," she says to me.

"But Mom!" I cry.

"I said, let's *go*."

As she drags me out into the evening sunshine, Mike follows.

"I work at Ted's Auto Repair, on Wilson Street," he calls out to me. "If you want to talk, you can find me there."

———

On the way home we're all quiet for a time. Everything about this familiar drive feels weird today, sort of unreal.

Then, from the back seat, Ella asks, "Why are you guys so mad at each other?"

Mom looks more scared than mad. I'm not sure what I'm feeling.

"You don't have to worry," Mom says to Ella. "Everything's okay."

But things are *not* okay. Dad isn't really my dad. Some stranger named Mike is. How do I make sense of that?

"Who was that man you were talking to?" Ella asks.

Mom glances back at her through the rear-view mirror. "Just someone I used to know," she says.

"Is he your friend?" Ella asks.

Mom stares back at the road. "No."

I look out the side window at the passing houses. My head is swirling with thoughts. Who is Mike? How did this happen? If Dad isn't my dad and Mike is, then who am I? I feel like my whole life is a lie. I'm a stranger to myself.

Chapter Three

Dad's truck isn't in the driveway when we park in front of the house. He's a salesperson, working for several companies. He's always on the road, often gone for days, sometimes weeks, at a time.

But he was supposed to be home this evening. He said he would come see me at the talent show.

"Let's have pizza tonight," Mom says as she unlocks the front door. "I don't feel like making dinner."

"Pizza!" Ella cries.

"Whatever," I say, following them into the house. After meeting Mike and finding out my dad isn't my real dad, I don't feel like eating. I dump the roses Mike gave me into the trash can by the door.

Tonight the house feels odd, like it's not really mine. It's that feeling you get when you come home after a long vacation, like you're walking into some stranger's house. Suddenly I'm noticing things I haven't before. The sour smell of the compost in the kitchen. The dust on the TV. How the one cushion on the couch sags, where Dad always sits.

As Mom phones for pizza delivery, I go into my bedroom. Even my room feels weird and sort of sad now. There are dust bunnies under my bed. The poster of a boy band I don't listen to anymore dangles from just one thumbtack. The clothes hanging in my closet seem glum. Half of them don't fit anymore.

I run a hand over my cheek as I look in the mirror. No wonder I don't have Dad's black curly hair or his brown eyes. My eyes are green, like Mike's. My hair is reddish brown and straight, like Mike's. I don't look anything like Dad. But I never really thought about it before because I'm so much like my mom. I have her heart-shaped face and long nose. I'm quick to get mad or sad, like her.

But I did always wonder why I'm so much taller than my parents. Now I know. I have long arms and legs, like Mike.

Is this really my home? If Dad isn't my dad, do I belong here? If not, where *do* I belong?

I flop on my bed and pull the pillow over my face. I scream into it.

When the pizza arrives, Mom and Ella eat at the table in silence. I eat standing up, leaning against the kitchen counter. But the pizza is greasy, and I feel sick. I drop the slice back onto my plate.

Then I hear Dad's truck in the driveway. Mom and I lock gazes. She looks scared, the way I feel. "You can't say anything to him," she says. About Mike being my father, she means.

"I *know*," I say. "I'm not stupid." If I told Dad about Mike, he'd likely leave us.

"You can't say anything about what?" Ella asks, her mouth full of pizza.

"Nothing," I say.

Dad walks into the kitchen, carrying his travel bag…and my roses. "Who dumped these flowers in the garbage?" he asks, setting down his bag.

Mom and I exchange another wide-eyed glance. How am I going to explain the flowers?

"Some guy gave them to Jen," Ella says.

Dad looks from Ella to me. "A boy gave you flowers?" he asks me. He looks surprised. "You've got a *boyfriend*?"

"No," I say, taking the flowers from him. I drop them in the kitchen garbage.

"Okay," Dad says slowly. "Did I hit a nerve?"

"Jen won third in the talent show," Mom says to change the subject.

Dad smacks his forehead. "I forgot all about it." He hugs me. "I'm so sorry I missed it, honey."

"Like you always do," I say. "Didn't you see my texts?"

"I was driving. I haven't checked for messages yet." He peers down at his phone now, scrolls through the texts. "I hit construction on the road earlier in the day. Waited in line forever."

I cross my arms. "You always have an excuse," I say.

"Jen, that's enough," Mom says. "How about we all just sit together and eat?" She offers Dad a slice of pizza.

I sit but don't eat. None of us says anything for a time.

Dad watches each of us in turn as he chews. Then he puts down his slice of pizza. "What's going on?" he asks.

Mom shrugs. "Nothing."

Ella wipes pizza sauce off her mouth with the back of her hand. "Mom and Jen had a fight," she says.

Dad lifts his chin as if he understands. "I really am sorry about missing the concert," he says to me. He must think that's why we were arguing. "I'll make it up to you. How about we catch a game this weekend?"

He smiles, and I'm sure he means well. But it seems like Dad doesn't really know me. What I like. What I don't like.

"I don't like watching baseball," I say. All that sitting while other people have fun. It's boring. I don't even like *playing* baseball—or any other organized sport. Music is my thing. I'd rather be singing.

Dad sits back in his chair. "You don't like baseball?" He seems surprised. And hurt. "But you went with me to all those games—"

"I went because *you* like it," I say. I wanted to spend time with my dad, and he's all about sports.

"*I* want to go to the game!" Ella says. Mostly for the hot dogs, I'm sure.

Dad taps Ella's nose, and my sister giggles. "You got it, button nose." That's Dad's nickname for Ella. He never gave me a nickname.

As I watch Dad joke with Ella, it occurs to me that Ella is his favorite. He's always gotten along better with my sister than he does with me. Now I know why. He's not really my dad.

My belly feels sick at the thought. I push back my chair and leave the table.

"Are you done eating?" Mom asks me.

"I'm not hungry."

"Clean up your mess then," she says.

I grab my plate and throw the pizza into the garbage on top of the roses. The lid of the garbage can bangs shut. I toss the dish into the sink, nearly breaking it.

"Go easy there," Dad says.

But I stomp down the hall.

Before I slam my bedroom door, I hear Dad say, "What's gotten into her?"

Chapter Four

In the morning I take a city bus to the car-repair shop where Mike works. So he is a mechanic. I wonder how he and Mom met. But I'm not about to ask Mike that. I'm here for only one reason. To tell Mike to stay away.

I storm through the big open doors of the shop. I can see Mike working under a car that is raised off the ground. He wears blue coveralls like the other mechanics here. They all turn when they see me march in.

"Jen!" Mike says. "You came! I wasn't sure you would."

"I won't let you ruin things," I say.

Mike wipes his dirty hands on a rag. "What do you mean?"

"That's what you want, isn't it?" I ask. "Why you turned up at my concert. You want to break up my mom and dad. Well, it's not going to work."

"I don't want to break up their marriage!" Mike says. He glances at the other men, who are listening. "Honestly, I just wanted to hear you sing."

"But you gave me those roses." If he hadn't, I never would have noticed him.

"I *was* hoping to meet you," he says. "But then I saw your mom and—" He stops to collect his thoughts. "There's so much I want to tell you, Jen. About your family—"

I cross my arms. "What about my family?"

"I mean my parents, your cousins, your—"

I cut him off. "You mean *your* family," I say. "I have a family of my own, my own grandparents and cousins. I already have a dad. And if he finds out about you, he'll leave us."

"I'm so sorry, Jen." Mike rubs a hand over his mouth. "I guess I didn't think things through. But I only wanted to meet you, to get to know you."

"If you wanted that so much," I say, "then why wait seventeen years?"

Mike leads me out of the garage, away from his co-workers. "Your mom didn't want me in your life," he says once we're outside. "Just like you said, she was afraid if your dad found out, that would be the end of their marriage. I didn't like it, but I had to respect her wishes."

I put my hands on my hips. "So why now? Why turn up out of the blue?"

"It wasn't out of the blue," he says. "Not for me. I've kept tabs on you through social media throughout the years. I watched you grow up from a baby into a beautiful young woman. You just turned seventeen. I figured you were old enough now to make your own choice, whether you want me in your life or not."

I cross my arms. "I don't."

Mike steps back as if I've taken a swing at him. I can tell he's hurt. "Okay," he says. "If that's the case, I'll respect that too."

"This is all for nothing then?" I ask. "You turn my life upside down and disappear again?"

Mike shakes his head. "Only if that's what you want. If you want me in your life, I'm here. If you don't, then I'll just have to accept that. But Jen, I *do* want to be in your life. I've always wanted that."

I look away, at the busy street. "Like I said, I don't want that." Or do I? There are so many things I want to know that only Mike can tell me. But then what would happen to our family? If Dad found out I was here with

Mike right now, he would almost certainly leave us. "Just stay away from me," I say.

Mike puts a hand on my arm. "Maybe take a little time to think about it," he says.

But I turn and walk away, talking over my shoulder. "I don't need to think about it. I have one dad, not two."

"What kind of ice cream do you like?" Mike calls out.

I turn. "What?"

"Ice cream," he says. "What's your favorite kind?"

I shrug. What's he getting at? "Mint chocolate chip."

Mike nods and grins. "I knew it. People either love it or hate it. I knew it would be your favorite."

"How?"

"Because it's mine."

Mike is right. People either love mint ice cream, or they hate it. The rest of my family hates it. Mom buys a tub of strawberry or chocolate for the three of them, and mint for me.

Mike walks toward me, pulling out his phone. "It's someone else's favorite too," he says.

"Yeah? Who?"

He scrolls through his photos and shows me one of himself and a boy about Ella's age. The kid looks just like Mike. Which is to say he looks a lot like me. Mike taps the picture. "My son, Jack," he says. "He loves mint ice cream too."

"I have a brother?"

Then I look back to the photo of Mike and Jack. They are both smiling. Behind them is a Christmas tree. The boy is holding out a gift, like he's offering it to me.

I feel the ground shift under my feet.

I have a brother.

Chapter Five

When I get home, Mom is waiting for me in the kitchen. She stands as I toss my backpack onto the table.

"Where were you?" she asks. "I texted—"

"Where's Dad?" I glance at the stairs that lead up to my parents' bedroom. "I see his truck is still in the yard."

"He's in the garage." She scans my face. "Why? What's happened?"

"I went to see Mike," I say.

Mom sinks back into her chair. "I was afraid you had."

"I have a brother, Mom. Did you know that?"

She nods slowly. "I heard Mike had married and then remarried."

"I have this whole other family," I say too loudly. "I just don't understand why you didn't tell me."

"You know why," she says. "Steve would have left me if I told him about Mike."

Mom and Dad argue a lot, mostly about how often Dad's on the road. Something like this *would* tear them apart.

"But it's not fair to me!" I yell. "Mom, Mike is my *father*. Jack is my *brother*. They are my *family*, and I have so many more relatives. You didn't allow me to get to know any of them."

"Please tell me you're not going to continue to see Mike," Mom says, and her voice also rises.

"But I have so many questions for him, about my family." I poke my own chest. "About *me*." About why I like the things I do, why I'm the way I am. "I never quite felt like I belonged in this family."

Mom puts a hand on my arm. "Oh, sweetheart. You *do* belong with us."

I pull away. "Maybe with you." *Sort of.*

"But not with Dad. Things were always awkward between us. You know I'm right."

"He has been impatient with you—"

"Like he doesn't really get me," I say.

"Steve loves you," Mom says. "You know he does."

"But would he love me if he found out Mike is my father?"

"Of course he would."

"Then tell him, Mom."

She shakes her head. "If I did, would he still love *me*?"

Just then we both hear Dad bang in through the front door.

"What's going on?" Dad asks. "I heard shouting."

"It's nothing," Mom says, turning away.

"It's *not* nothing," I cry. And then I just can't take it anymore. If she's not going to tell him, I will. "I met somebody last night," I say to Dad. "The guy who gave me those flowers."

"*Jen*," Mom says. "Please, no."

"His name is Mike," I say. I pause.

Dad nods. "And..."

"And he says he's my father."

Dad squints at me. "Say that again?"

"A guy named Mike told me he is my real dad."

Dad looks at Mom. Her head is down.

"Sara," Dad says to Mom. "Can I have a word? In private?"

I know what that means. My parents are about to argue again.

And this time, it's my fault.

From the kitchen I can hear Mom and Dad arguing upstairs in their bedroom. Their raised voices boom. Dad's angry about Mom's affair with Mike, even though it happened eighteen years ago. Mom's trying to explain. It's a mess.

It's *my* mess. I caused this. I should never have told Dad about Mike.

Worse, I should never have been born. I wouldn't have been if Mom hadn't had that affair with Mike. I lean over the table and hold my head in my hands.

Then it occurs to me that if I can hear every word Mom and Dad are saying, so can Ella.

I rush down the hall to Ella's room. But then I hover at her door a moment before knocking. How am I going to handle this? Finally I knock. When Ella doesn't answer, I open her door. "Ella?"

I find her wedged between her bed and the wall, hugging a teddy bear. She's been crying.

I sit on the floor with her. Then I point up at the ceiling. "I guess you heard what Mom and Dad are fighting about?"

Ella nods. How could she not hear? Their voices are even louder now. Their bedroom is right above Ella's.

"Is that guy who gave you the roses really your dad?" she asks.

"Yes."

She hugs her teddy bear a little tighter. "You do kind of look like him," she says.

And Ella looks like *her* dad, Steve. She's short, with black curly hair and brown eyes. Her skin tans beautifully in the summer. My pale skin just burns in the sun.

"Does that mean we aren't sisters?" she asks.

"We *are* sisters," I say. I pause to think about that. "Half sisters, I guess."

"But not full ones. Like before." She wipes the tears from her eyes with her sleeve.

I wrap my arms around Ella. She's right. Things will never be quite the same.

"Dad says he wants to leave," she says. "*Is* he going to leave us?"

"I don't know."

A door slams. I hear Dad's footsteps thumping down the stairs. Ella and I scramble to the kitchen as he marches down the hall toward the front door. He's carrying his travel bag.

We both chase after him. "Where are you going?" Ella asks.

"A hotel."

"You're leaving us?" I ask.

Dad stops to run a hand through his hair. "I just need some time," he says. "To think."

Ella throws herself at him, wrapping her arms around his waist. "Daddy, don't go."

"When will you be back?" I ask.

"I don't know." Dad puts down his bag to hug Ella.

"But you *are* coming back, right?" I ask. "You're not moving out, are you?"

Dad doesn't answer. Still holding Ella, he cups my cheek with his hand. "I'm so sorry I wasn't there to see you sing last night," he says. "I should have been there for all your shows."

Then he picks up his bag and walks out the door, closing it behind him.

Chapter Six

The next morning is Sunday, our sleep-in morning. But Mom knocks on the door early, too early. It doesn't matter. I'm already awake. I didn't sleep much last night.

"Can I come in?" she asks.

I rub my eyes. "Yeah, I guess."

She closes the door and sits on the bed beside me. She's wearing the same clothes she had on last night. And she looks exhausted, like she didn't sleep either. I can tell she's been crying. But then, I've been crying too.

"How are you doing, sweetheart?" she asks.

"I've been better."

Mom looks down at her hand, fiddling with a fold in the sheets. "I'm sorry I couldn't be there for you last night."

"I understand."

"Thanks for sitting up with Ella."

"She's pretty upset."

She nods slowly. "We all are."

I tilt my head to get her to look at me. "Mom, is Dad leaving us for good?"

"I don't know," she says.

I feel my chin quiver as my eyes sting.

"Doesn't he love us anymore?"

"Oh, sweetheart," Mom says. She runs a hand over my hair. "Of course he loves you."

But I'm not even his daughter. "He's leaving because of me," I say.

Mom takes my hand. "No, he's leaving because of *me*," she says. "What I did eighteen years ago."

"But that's *so* long ago," I say.

She nods. "Yes, it is."

"Then it *is* because of me," I say. "If I hadn't been born, none of this would be happening now."

Mom wraps her arms around me. "Please don't think like that," she says. "None of this is your fault."

I don't believe her. And either way, Dad left.

"I just don't understand how you could keep this a secret for so long," I say.

Mom lets out a long sigh. "I was afraid Steve would leave me over it. And now he has. But I guess I was more afraid of losing you. I wanted you here, with me."

I sit a little straighter. "You were scared I'd go live with Mike?" There *were* times when I wished I could move out. When the arguments between Mom and Dad got bad. But would I have moved in with Mike? Maybe, if I had grown up knowing him.

"I was wrong," Mom says. "I can see that now. I should have told Steve about Mike. And Mike should have been a part of your life." She takes my hand again. "I think he would have been a good dad too."

But I pull my hand from her grip. "Why did you start seeing Mike in the first place?" I ask. "I mean, you had only been married to Dad a couple of years, right?"

Mom nods. "Things were always bumpy between Steve and me. He was away so much with work. I started to feel like his job mattered more to him than I did."

I snort. "I know the feeling."

Mom smiles a little. "And then I met Mike. A friend took me to a pub where Mike was playing onstage. A solo act. Just him and his guitar. He sang his own songs, ones he had written."

"He's a *musician*?" I try to fit the image of that grubby mechanic I saw yesterday with a guitarist onstage. "He *sings*?" Just like me.

"He didn't tell you?" Mom asks.

"We didn't talk that much." I left right after he showed me the picture of him and his son.

"He's a really good musician," Mom says. "And he's got a beautiful singing voice. You clearly got your talent and love of music from him."

She's right. Mom can't carry a tune. And Dad? Let's just say that when he sings in the shower, the rest of us have giggle fits.

"When I found out I was pregnant," Mom says, "I knew you were Mike's baby. The timing. Steve had been away when—"

I put my hands to my ears. "I don't want to hear about it."

Mom sits back. "But I had a home with Steve. I didn't want my marriage to end." She wipes tears from her eyes. "I begged Mike to leave us alone. He didn't want to, but he did. For me."

I slump back against my pillow. "I was a mistake then."

Mom lifts my chin so I'll look at her. "Oh, Jen," she says. "I made a lot of poor decisions in my life. But you aren't one of them. I wanted you, sweetheart. You were a gift. The biggest gift."

Maybe. I'm just not convinced Dad feels the same way.

***

I stay in bed for a while after Mom leaves, trying to fall back asleep. When I can't, I finally get up to use the bathroom. As I walk down the hall, I hear Ella crying in her bedroom. I push her door open to see her lying on her bed, hugging a stuffie. "Hey," I say.

But she rolls over, turning her back to me. I sit on the bed next to her. "Are you okay?"

She wipes her nose on her sleeve. "What do you think?" she says.

"What's going on?"

She glares back at me like I should know. And I do.

"Dad's gone," she says.

"And what?" I ask. "You want me to feel bad for being born?" Like I don't already.

"You didn't have to tell Dad about Mike."

It *is* my fault. Maybe Mom should have told Dad I was Mike's daughter years ago. But I opened my big mouth and told him myself.

And then he left.

I've got to find a way to bring him home and pull my family back together again. I need to fix this.

Chapter Seven

When I knock on the hotel door, Dad opens it right away. He's expecting me. I texted him earlier to say I was coming. The hotel room is dated, a bit scruffy. A big queen-sized bed sits in the middle of the room.

"Come in, Jen," he says. "Would you like something to drink? I have orange juice in the mini fridge." He's being so polite—*too* polite.

Like we're strangers. Seeing him in this awful hotel room, it feels like we are. Like I don't really know him. And he doesn't know me. I mean, I don't even like orange juice.

I shake my head. I'm not here to visit or make small talk. I get right to the point. "Did you leave because of me?" I ask him. "Because I'm Mike's daughter?"

"Oh, honey, no," Dad says. "That's not it at all. I left because I'm mad your mom lied to me. And she kept on lying to me. Sara never told me about Mike, or that he was your father. If she had, things might have been different." He pauses. "The weird thing is, I think some part of me already knew."

"How?" I ask. "Because I'm so different from you?"

"Maybe a little. We've always butted heads. I never felt like I could connect with you—"

He stops there, so I finish the sentence for him. "Like you can connect with Ella." I slump into a chair. "Ella *is* your favorite."

Dad sits on the end of the bed. "It's not like that," he says. "I don't have a favorite."

"Don't you?" I ask. "If you knew I was Mike's daughter, would you have raised me anyway?"

"Yes, of course I would have."

"Would it have been the same? Would you have thought of me in the same way, as your daughter?"

Dad hesitates just a moment too long before answering. So I know he's not sure about that either. "Yes, I would have thought of you as my daughter," he says finally.

But would I have been the same person? If Mike had been in my life from the start, who would I be now? Would I have lived with him? Probably, at least part of the time. Mom said Mike is a musician. He likely would have taught me everything he knows. I wouldn't have felt like an outsider in my own family. I might have felt like I belonged.

"If some part of you knew I wasn't your daughter, did you love me less because of it?" I ask Dad. "Is that why you missed so many of my concerts?"

"What? No! Jen, I missed the concerts because I'm on the road so much with my job. I work hard to make sure my family has a nice place to live, and everything you need. And so you and Ella have money to go to college after you graduate. I want you to have the things I didn't have when I was growing up."

"I thought maybe—" I try to stop myself from crying. "I thought it was because you don't love me. Not the way you love Ella."

Dad leans forward and takes both of my hands. He looks up at me as he talks. "I love you, Jen. I've always loved you."

"Then come home," I say. "Can't things go back to the way they were?"

"I'm not sure they can. I can't ignore what's happened."

I pull my hands from his. "So that's it? You're never coming home?"

Dad sighs as he sits back. "I don't know, honey. Right now I'm feeling really hurt.

I need some time to think about who I am and what I want. Now that things have changed."

I wipe my eyes and nod slowly as I push myself out of my chair. I have to figure that out for myself too.

"But you're still my dad, right?" I ask.

He stands and hugs me. "That's never going to change," he says. "I'll always be your dad." He steps back to look at me. "If you want me to be."

"Of course I do," I say. "Why would you even say that?"

He shrugs. "Like you said, I haven't always been there for you, any more than I have for your mother. I can understand why you might want to give up on me. Maybe Mike would be a better father."

"Nobody could be a better dad than you," I say.

He shoves his hands in the pockets of his jeans. "Have you seen Mike?" he asks. "Have you talked with him?"

"Not much," I say. "I stopped in at his repair shop. Mostly to tell him to leave us alone. But then—" I hug myself. "I've got a brother, Dad. And Mike is a musician. He sings onstage, like me. He even likes mint chocolate chip ice cream, like I do."

Dad nods sadly. "I guess it's only natural that you would have more in common with him than you do with me."

And then I finally get it. Dad is worried that Mike will take me away from him.

"I think I want to get to know Mike," I say. "I guess in part because that will help me know myself." I take his hand. "But you're my dad."

"Not your birth father," he says.

"No. But you were there when I took my first steps." I squeeze his hand. "You taught me how to ride my bike. When I broke my arm, you put up that huge banner in front of the house welcoming me home from the hospital."

Dad grins. "You told me to take it down before anyone from school saw it."

"But I still loved that you did that."

Dad takes my other hand. "No matter what happens between your mom and me," he says,

"I'm going to stay in your life. I'm not going to disappear."

"We miss you, Dad. Mom, Ella and me. We all miss you."

He wraps his arms around me. "I miss you too."

"Things *are* changing, aren't they?" I say into his shoulder.

"Yes, they are."

"I'm scared," I say.

He squeezes me harder. "Me too."

Chapter Eight

A week after Dad moved into that cheap hotel, I arrive home from school to find Mom getting ready to go out. She's wearing a red dress, sandals and gold hoop earrings.

"You look nice," I say as I enter the kitchen. "Where are you going?"

"I was just about to text you," she says. "Do you mind babysitting Ella tonight?"

65

"I'm not sure she'll want me to," I say. "Ella hasn't really talked to me since Dad left." I drop my backpack on the floor. "In any case, Mike asked me to come over to his place tonight."

"Maybe you can go to Mike's another day." Mom slips on her jacket. "Jen, this is important. Dad invited me out to supper, to talk."

"Does that mean he's coming home?" I ask.

"I wish I could say yes, but I don't think so. Not yet anyway."

I wave at the door. "Go. I'll take care of Ella."

Mom gives me a quick hug. "Thanks, sweetheart." She slings her purse over her shoulder as she leaves the house.

I sigh as I pick up my backpack and carry it down the hall. I'm not sure Ella's ever going to forgive me for telling Dad about Mike. But we have to start talking again sometime.

I knock on her door. "Ella?"

She doesn't answer. I open her door anyway.

She rolls over on her bed to look at me. "I didn't say you could come in," she says.

I drop my backpack at the door. "Mom just left," I say. "She's having dinner with Dad tonight."

"I know," Ella says. "She told me."

I sit on the bed next to her. "I'm sorry about everything that happened, about Dad leaving."

Ella turns away from me.

"But I know now that it isn't my fault Dad left," I say. "That's between him and Mom. Not you and me."

Ella doesn't respond.

"Are you ever going to talk to me again?" I ask.

Without looking at me, she shakes her head, her pigtails dangling. "No."

I raise my eyebrows and smile a little. "Would you talk to me if I bought you a burger and fries?"

She looks at me over her shoulder. "Maybe."

"How about if I bought you ice cream too?" I ask.

She sits up to face me. "Strawberry?"

"Any flavor you like."

"But not mint chocolate chip," she says.

"No," I say. "That's what *I'll* get."

"I hate mint."

"I love it."

She looks down at her lap. "Are you really still my sister?" she asks.

"Of course I am." I take her hand. "I'll never stop being your sister. And Dad won't stop being our dad. We're still a family, Ella."

"Even if Dad doesn't live with us?" she asks.

"Even then." I stand and pull her up. "Come on," I say. "Let's go grab a burger."

"And ice cream?"

"And ice cream."

I pick up my backpack as I lead her out the door. "Once we've eaten," I say, "there's someone I'd like you to meet."

After our supper out, Ella and I take the bus to the address Mike texted me. Mike's house is small and old, but it's freshly painted. There's a flower garden out front. I knock on the door.

A boy opens it, and I recognize him from the photo Mike showed me. It's Jack, my brother. But he doesn't recognize me at first. He calls over his shoulder, "Dad, somebody's here."

In a moment Mike is behind him. "Well, hello!" he says to both me and Ella. He puts a hand on his son's shoulder. "Jack, this is Jen, your sister."

"He's your *brother*?" Ella looks up at me, wide-eyed.

"Nice to finally meet you," Jack says. He holds out his hand.

I laugh a little as I shake his—he sounds and acts like a grown-up. But he's the same age as Ella, nine. "It's good to meet you too," I say. "Jack, this is Ella, my sister."

"Jack's all about *Minecraft*," Mike says.

"Me too," Ella says.

Jack waves her inside. "Come on," he says. "You can check out the castle I built."

And just like that, they're gone.

"I think Jack's made a new friend," Mike says as I step into the living room.

"He's a cool kid," I say. "Smart."

Mike grins. "Like his big sister."

I smile back shyly. Then I point at a guitar leaning against a chair. "Is this your guitar?"

"One of them."

"How many do you have?"

"A few." He leads me down the hall. "Come with me. I've got something for you."

Mike goes into a room. When I join him inside, I see it's a music room. Guitars hang from the walls. There's a mic on a stand. And beside that, on a large desk, a keyboard and computer, a setup for recording. "Cool," I say.

Mike picks up a guitar. "Here," he says, handing it to me. "This is for you."

I take the guitar from him. "You mean I can keep it?"

"It's yours."

"Wow. Thanks!" Still standing, I begin to strum. "I always wanted to play the guitar."

"I can teach you," Mike says. "Come over for weekly lessons. More often, if you want. It would give us a chance to talk. Get to know each other."

I nod as I check out the guitar. "I'd like that." Then I feel a pang of guilt in my stomach. Will Dad feel bad about me spending time with Mike? From what he said in the hotel room, I think he might. But I really want to learn how to play the guitar. And I want to get to know Mike. He's my dad too.

I glance at the family photo on the desk. Mike, Jack and a pretty woman in a black dress. "Your wife won't mind me coming over so often?" I ask.

Mike smiles. "I've already talked to her about it."

"She knows about me?" I ask.

"I told her about you not long after I met her." Mike points at a stool, inviting me to take a seat. "She'd like you to come to dinner next Sunday, by the way. You can bring your sister again. Jack would like that."

I think about Dad again. "I'll have to see," I say.

Mike picks up his guitar and sits on another stool next to me. "Let me show you a few chords," he says.

As he teaches me, I keep thinking, This guy is my dad. My *dad*. I have *two* fathers. How weird is that? How *cool* is that?

And all at once I understand that no matter what happens now between Mom and Dad, my family isn't going to get smaller. It's only gotten bigger.

Chapter Nine

A year later, the stage lights are in my eyes. But my knees no longer shake. I feel confident in front of the audience now. With the mic in my hands, I lift my voice to the sky.

Every Wednesday night musicians play on this outdoor stage near the wharf. And this evening it's my turn. It's a gig, a job, that Mike got for me. In fact, he's sitting behind me onstage, playing the guitar as I sing. It's one of several shows we've performed together over the last year.

On the grass below, Mike's wife and my brother, Jack, watch from lawn chairs. Not far away, Mom, Dad and Ella sit together. Dad grins at me when I glance his way, encouraging me as I sing.

Mom and Dad arrived separately. They are still living apart. But they are seeing each other. They're going to a marriage counselor, trying to work things out. And it seems to be helping. At least they don't argue so much anymore.

But I think that's mostly because Dad took a desk job so he's not traveling all the time. We see more of him now than we did when he lived with us. We hang out almost every weekend, and he drops in for supper throughout the week. He hasn't missed one of my concerts. I've been getting to know him all over again. And in a way, I've also been getting to know myself.

When I first met Mike, I thought I must be more like him than my dad. After all, he is my natural father. I would have inherited traits, like being good at music, from him.

But now I get just how much of myself also came from Dad, from Steve, since he raised me. I got my corny sense of humor from him. And I always go barefoot in the house, like Dad, even though Mom nags us both to wear socks or slippers. Dad and I both really love black licorice. (I found out

Mike *hates* it.) And Dad is really into horror movies, just like me.

There has been a lot to get used to this past year. I met a whole other family I didn't know I had. And things are about to change again. I graduate in June. And in the fall I'll be moving onto a campus in Vancouver, where I'm taking a music program. I won't have to work a part-time job, either, as Dad saved enough money for my schooling.

Once I leave, I won't see so much of either one of my families. But that's okay. I know they'll always be there. I know where I belong—with both of them.

I finish my song. It's the last one of our set. I take a bow, then turn to Mike so he'll take a bow too. When I look back, my dad, Steve, has stepped up to the stage. He hands me a single rose, as he has at the end of each of my concerts. I take it from him and sniff it. Then, not just for this rose but for everything he's done for me, I mouth a single word. *Thanks.*

Author's Note

Like Jen, I grew up with one father, only to find out later that I also had a natural, or birth, father. My own story is very different from the one you read here, but I do know what it's like to discover, in your teens, that you have a whole other family.

For me, that discovery raised a lot of questions, many that Jen explores in this book. Was I still a part of my existing family? Who was I now?

As I got to know my birth father, I found that I shared many specific tastes and traits with him. And yet, even years after both dads have passed away, I dream of the dad I grew up with. It's his voice that counsels me now that I have four children of my own.

My birth dad gave me my genetic makeup, which differs in many ways from those of my half sisters. But the dad who raised me influenced me hugely and helped shape the person I am today.

So here's to our families, and all the varied shapes and forms they take, the homes they make and the people we become within them.

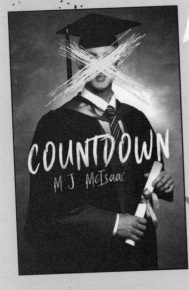

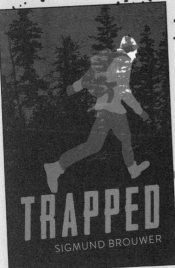

TRAPPED

SIGMUND BROUWER

WHAT SEEMS LIKE A DREAM COME TRUE QUICKLY TURNS INTO A NIGHTMARE.

A HIGH-STAKES INTERNET REALITY SHOW SET ON A DESERTED ISLAND...WHAT COULD GO WRONG?

DROPPED!

ALICE KUIPERS